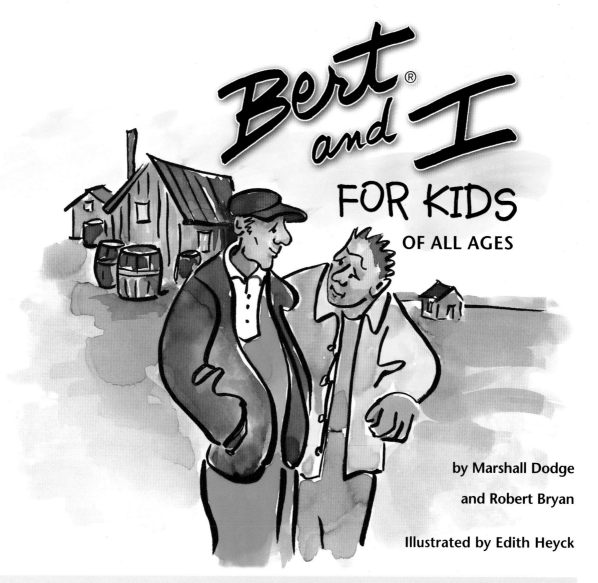

Bert and I ®
and I
FOR KIDS
OF ALL AGES

by Marshall Dodge

and Robert Bryan

Illustrated by Edith Heyck

• Tales From Down East •

*Dedicated to all Down East storytellers,
young and not-so-young.*

Published by **Down East Books** / Camden, Maine

BY A FLUKE

Bert and I come down to the dock around six o'clock in the morning.

Bert went into the bait shack to get some pot warp, and I went down on the dock to start up the *Bluebird.*

I closed the porcelain switch on the old Knox one-lunger, opened up the fuel line, primed the cylinder, and Bert started crankin' her over.

Sa∗ha   Sa∗ha
Sa∗ha
Pum Pum. Be

Pum Pum Pum. Be
   Pum Pum Pum. Be
Pum Pum Pum. Be

She fired right up on the first try.

Most folks think she runs kinda rough, but that is just the way they make them old make-and-break one-lungers. Sometimes they don't fire for ten strokes, but the flywheel is heavy enough to carry them in between.

"Cast off, Bert."

Bert cast off the mooring line, and the *Bluebird* made off to Ledyard Point.

Pum Pum Pum. Be

Pum Pum Pum. Be

When we come out from under the lee of the land we commenced to roll somethin' fierce, so we put up the steadyin' sail.

Sscrreeeeeccchhhh Then, right out
in the middle of the channel,
we run aground.

Hard.

So hard, in fact, we stove in the boat.

When the rock we had struck hove up alongside of us, we could see it was...

a whale!

We must have
knocked him out
when we hit him,
'cause he just lay
there and wallowed
in the waves.

As the *Bluebird* went down under us, we jumped up on top of the whale and stuck the mast of the steadyin' sail in his blowhole.

We swung the whale off the wind and headed for home on a broad reach.

Sssshhhhhhh

"Hard to port, Bert."

Bert put us hard to port by twistin' the tail of the whale, and we sailed into our little harbor nice as you please.

But all them waves splashing over the front end of the whale revived him enough so that he begun to stir about!

"Steady on, Bert, only a hundred yards more."

Aaacchhooooo

Just as we nosed up
on the rocks
in front
of the bait shack,
the whale sneezed.

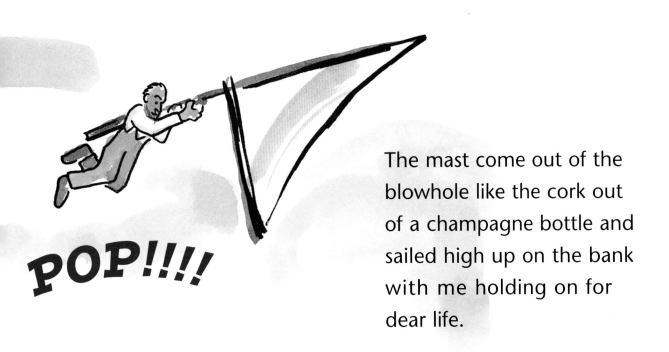

POP!!!!

The mast come out of the blowhole like the cork out of a champagne bottle and sailed high up on the bank with me holding on for dear life.

The whale awoke and flipped Bert...

...high up in a tree,
where he stayed,
refusing to come down.

"Come on down outta that tree, Bert," I cried!
"We lost our boat, and the whale got away,
but no use sulkin'! We got to lay the keel for
the NEW *Bluebird*. Don't want the species
to die out, do you?"

The Pet Turkey

When I was a boy, my father gave me a turkey chick to raise and fatten for Christmas dinner. He grew into a fine, fat gobbler. And just before Christmas, my father told me to kill the bird, pluck him, and clean him.

Well, I looked at the turkey.

And he looked at me.

And I told my father I'd wait
a little bit longer.

Come Christmas Eve,
Father told me I'd have
to kill the bird, or he would.

I looked at the bird.

And he looked at me.

And I told Father that I'd take care
of it after Father had gone to bed.

Later, I got out the axe,
and I looked at the bird.

And he looked at me.

And I didn't have the
heart to kill him.

So, I fed him
hard cider and
I plucked him,
and I put him in
the 'fridgeator.

Next morning when Father opened up
the 'fridgeator door, that turkey came out
a-struttin' all over the kitchen floor, proud
and naked as the day he was born.

And you know, we never did kill that bird.

My father and me, we spent the rest of
Christmas day knittin' him a sweater!

Gagnon Champion Moose Caller

Oui, monsieur,
I am Gagnon,
World
Champion
Moose
Caller.

Already when I am born,
I am champion moose caller.
I let out my first holler
in that little cabin in
the Allagash –

AaaaooOOO

and three moose,
they walk in through
the door!

WWWwwooooo

I reach the age of twelve, and the governor of the state of Maine, he ask me to make a moose count for him. He knows I am the only man in the world who can get all the moose in Maine together at one time.

AaaaooOOO

I climb up Mt. Katahdin, to the highest peak in the state, and I let out my moose holler.

As soon as it bounce off Cadillac Mountain and make echo off Mars Hill, everywhere there is a cloud of dust. I have to climb rock so I don't get stomped to death!

But, from this perch I count 342,698 moose, 5 Alaska caribou, and a dog with Hawaiian license tag.

Oui, monsieur, I am Gagnon, *World Champion Moose Caller.*

Last year when
I retire, I am asked
to New York to
show a group
of sportsmen
how I make
my holler.

I am scared about what
will happen, even though
I take out moose insurance.

After the dinner, I get up
and give my moose call.

Well, as soon as it strike
Radio City, hit Empire State
and bounce back from the
Statue of Liberty, we hear a
clatter of hoof in hallway.

NWooooo

And doors fly open
to show, first, ugly nose.
Then mournful eyes.
Then massive rack, the powerful forequarters, huge hindquarters
of eight-foot-tall bull moose, pawing the red plush carpet!

These sportsmen,

HA!

they dive behind
tables and chairs.

But I let out a little
moose whimper,

aaaooOOO

and the moose, he walk over
into the corner, where he
stand as quiet as a baby.

Next morning, I take him with
me on the train back to Maine.
When I lead the moose into the
woods I see he walk stiff-legged,
and I could have sware I see
sawdust trickle out of one ear.

Sure enough, two days later I receive a letter from one of those sportsmen in which there is a clipping from the *New York Times* reporting the strange disappearance of the moose from the glass case at the Natural History Museum.

Oui, monsieur, I am Gagnon, *World Champion Moose Caller.*

ISBN 0-89272-580-X
Library of Congress Control Number: 2002103526

Printed in China

5   4   3   2   1

Down East Books / Camden, Maine
Book orders: 1-800-766-1670
www.downeastbooks.com